THIS BOOK BELONGS TO:

Other Kipper books

Kipper
Kipper's Toybox
Kipper's Birthday
Kipper's Snowy Day
Kipper's Christmas Eve
Where, Oh Where, is Kipper's Bear?
Kipper's Book of Colours
Kipper's Book of Opposites
Kipper's Book of Counting
Kipper's Book of Weather

Swing!

Mick Inkpen

Hodder
Children's
Books

A division of Hodder Headline Limited

Kipper and Tiger had
found a rope hanging
from a tree. On the end was
a stick for a seat.

'Look at me!' said Kipper.
'I can swing!'

'Look at me!' said Tiger.
'I can spin!'

But Kipper wasn't
watching. He was too busy
trying to stand on his head.

Kipper couldn't stand
on his head.
   So Tiger tried, while
Kipper balanced the stick
on his nose.

'I can't stand on
my head either,'
said Tiger. 'But I
can do a cartwheel!
Look!'

They could both walk the tightrope, in a wobbly sort of way.

'We should be in the circus!' said Tiger.

W hen Pig came along,
they showed him all
their tricks.

'Can you do
this?' said
Kipper.

B ut Pig couldn't.
He couldn't swing.
He couldn't spin.
He couldn't do cartwheels,
or balance a stick,
or walk the tightrope.

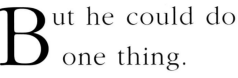

ut he could do
one thing.

He could stand on
his head. Perfectly.
For ages and ages.
And so could Arnold.

First published 2000
by Hodder Children's Books,
a division of Hodder Headline Limited,
338 Euston Road, London NW1 3BH

Copyright © Mick Inkpen 2000

10 9 8 7 6 5 4 3 2 1

ISBN 0 340 75420 6

A catalogue record for this book
is available from the British Library.
The right of Mick Inkpen to be identitfied
as the author of this Work
has been asserted by him in
accordance with the Copyright,
Designs and Patents Act 1988.

Printed in Hong Kong